Courage to Win

By
Steve Sutherland

Chapter 1 Diamondbacks
Spring Training

Chapter 2 Learning The Game

Chapter 3 Rotating Positions

Chapter 4 Finding Second Base

Chapter 5 Facing The Pitcher

Chapter 6 Developing My Swing

Chapter 7 Batting Cage

Chapter 8 Getting Beaned

Chapter 9 My First Hit

Chapter 10 Stealing Bases

Chapter 11 Early Seasons

Chapter 12 Pop Flies

Chapter 13 Middle Season

Chapter 14 Season End

Chapter 15 Playoffs

Chapter 16 Courage To Win

Chapter 1
Diamondbacks Spring Training

I seemed to be daydreaming out the school window. I could hardly wait for our first practice tonight. It seemed like every class was dragging. Even my teacher seemed to get lost in the noise in my head. Mom always starts our day with a prayer and a devotional. Those stories for some reason seem to stick with me all day. They make sense and I understand the rules. When I'm at school the rules seem to vary with the varying subjects that vary each day and the homework varies a bit it must not vary for a parental signature everyday. So, at least that is sticking with me. Baseball doesn't vary in my mind for some reason. It is so very clear. I remember very vividly the first time my Dad took us to Wrigley Field. We walked up those stadium stairs, which for my little feet at the time, seemed like two hundred thousand and fifty-three and a half steps. Then we reached are section of seats and we found ourselves looking past some cement walls that looked like a triangle and gave a glimpse of the most beautiful sight I have ever seen to date.

The inside of Wrigley Field is perhaps the most breath taking sight I have ever seen. The Baseball field was so clear and crisp the bases laid perfectly along the sand with green grass, which goes miles into the outfield. You almost feel the world spin as you approach your seats through those defining walls to a place that feels better than home. I could envision my self-running the bases after a spectacular hit. That day I have been told I learned my first lesson with sound. Sammy Sosa ripped a baseball out of the park and the crowd roared and it scared me horribly. Now if I heard that crowd roar again I would know that it is a very good thing and I would join in the roar with them, that's for sure. I like to remember it like a nice dream. It seems like I can go back there almost at will and feel that at home feeling whenever I want. So, here I find myself treading water through each of the varying subjects of my day in hope Mom will pick me up soon and I will have a quick snack, do my homework. Dad will come home I'll have just a little dinner and we will high tail it over to our first practice to meet all the boys and Coach Tyack and Coach Farina.

I believe I need to get going now and figure out what I'm suppose to learn today as I get through this arduous day. I can still see a glimmer of what tonight might hold. You have to give me that! Like, a fresh glass of water, to quench my thirst for my first practice with the new team.

Well, I made it through school, had my snack, I got my homework done, had an awesome dinner with my family. We're pulling out the driveway with my mitt and bat and Dad's smiling at me in the rear view mirror. What's that all about? Dad can we get there already! I'm trying to Andrew; we should be there soon. We pulled up to the curb and parked and I could see some boys gathering by the home plate. I opened my door and told Dad to come on and we ran toward home plate and met my fellow players and my coaches.

The coaches were busy getting the bases and pitchers mound out of the lock box for the baseball field. The were measuring out the bases from home plate to first base, then to third and finally the crucial second base. Second base needs to align with the pitchers mound and home plate and be centered between first base and third base.

The boys were all gathered together introducing themselves and showing each other their baseball mitts and bats. One of the boys introduced himself as Sam the coach's son and passed out the new team hats, the Diamondbacks. Andrew always loved getting his new hat and it literally became a commonality of belonging to a team and being able to contribute all he had inside of himself. The coach's begun to come in with their base gear and welcomed the boys to the Diamondback team. He numbered the boys of at random one-two, one-two until he ran out of boys. Andrew was a two and they were up at bat first. The coaches introduced themselves as Coach Tyack and Coach Farina. But, before they left all the boys were to tell each other what their names were, Evan, Adam, Brian, Sam, Joe, Danny, Alex, Andrew, Thomas, Brian, Zack and Tim, Coach Farina's son. Little did the boys know what would be their foundation for a new year of baseball for all of them? Most of the boy's have played two to three years. This was Andrews second season and I could just tell he loved it. You see it in his step, enthusiasm. Andrew would hang on every word the coach, or other team players would share with him. So, enough with the fanfare, it was time to play baseball. The two's ran up to get a batting helmet and their bats to begin practice. The coaches set the ones up on the infield. Some boys were at first, some at second, some were at short and the rest at third base. Coach Tyack was pitching and Coach Vince was catching for now. Coach Tyack had a nice big bucket of balls to go to for what looked like batting practice.

Evan was first at bat and was a lefty and he had some nice swings. Tim was a right handed, batter and looked pretty good. Andrew came up to bat at slammed the first pitch right back at coach and up the middle of the field. I loved the surprised look from his Coach Tyack. Andrew set himself up for his next at bat. The first pitch came in high and tight. Which, immediately had Andrew back up so he wouldn't get hit. Andrew got beamed in the back when he was on the Astro's and knew not to turn away from the pitch. Coach Tyack called for a baseball bat from the dugout. He had Andrew line up himself with the home plate again and put the bat behind him. He asked Andrew to stay in the batters box and not to back up. He should step forward, to hit the ball. Andrew set himself up for his third at bat and the coach through one outside, which he fouled off to the right. Andrew set up for his forth pitch that came in just perfect and hit it up the third base line. The coach nodded at him and said, "Next batter!" So, all in all, it wasn't a bad first at bat. It was great way to get the season rolling today. Andrew smiled at me and pulled off his batting helmet and the batting glove. He grabbed his new Diamondbacks hat and his baseball mitt and ran out to second base to catch some grounders from the other boys as they bat. Andrew knew if the ball came to him there he would throw it first base to get the out. So, Andrew made his way behind the other boys for his turn to field the ball if it came to him. Sam was in front of him and liked to play second too. Sam had a ball hit to him and he threw it to first for any easy out. Zack beat out the throw. Andrew set up nice and low watching the batter Danny as he was taught and the ball was hit to short. Andrew ran to second tag the base and made a great throw to first but Danny was safe. The boy's been starting to show some of their fight and will to win early in practice. Which had the

 The coaches were nodding at each other with smiles on each of their faces. They were in deed a competitive bunch of boy's who came to play. Andrew looked at me smiled and pulled his hat down over his eyes in a bashful way. He had a sense of pride and humility all at once. I love to watch him learn this great game and feel good about himself. Baseball can have a way at times of evening things out on the field. You feel the reverse sometimes. So, glory in the glory days and shake off the bad ones. The twilight skies were beginning to show the signs of robbing this fun filled day a way. Coach Tyack yelled out, "Great first practice!" Coach Vince echoed his thoughts as well. He yelled to the boys to bring in the bases and the pitcher mound and bring them to the lock box. Andrew grabbed his mitt and bat to get ready to go. Danny came up and slapped him on the head and said, "Nice practice Andrew!" Andrew smiled and pulled his hat down over his eyes again! He answered back, "You too Danny!" We walked side by side to the car quietly and reflected on a great first practice. We both opened the doors to the car and threw his baseball stuff in the car and headed home! I looked in The mirror again, to see a genuine smile on his face that only baseball seems to bring to Andrew. When we got home Andrew knew the routine and headed up to bed and kicked off his baseball pants and jumped into bed. Mom hollered out, "How did it go buddy?" Andrew said, "Good, Mom." We all know well it was his way of saying this is a game I love and can't wait to play the next day! Andrew put his head on the pillow and was humming himself to sleep. We smiled to each other and knew how great a day he had at his first practice. Not to mention his new Diamondbacks hat was hung up on his loft in the first position hook ready to wear when the next practice came. Baseball never varies. Practice and games go on every week until the seasons complete.

Chapter 2
Learning The Game

Initially, I believe in my talent. I know the skills I posses and the ground I need to cover in baseball. That is a fantastic place to start. I have some history to draw on even though this is my third year in little league. Baseball is still fresh and new to me. I enjoy the practice times and I love the games. The practice times give you that hone in on your skills and grow through the miscues to become a more complete baseball player. I listen to my coaches to the best of my ability. I like to think of it as simple as building blocks. I'm building on what I know and moving my abilities to the next level. I know stretching is a priority in the beginning of my baseball day. I need to stretch before every practice and especially if it is game day for our team. I know the next step is to begin throwing with someone else from a shorter distance and increase the distances while increase the speed at a comfortable level to make successful plays and execution. The throws must be concise to the point where the other player can catch the ball in a reasonable circumference to his glove and pull the ball out of the baseball glove and make a similar concise throw back to me. I believe that showing your fellow player respect gives him the best chance to make a successful play.

I love to run! Sometimes, the best release after a full day of reading, writing and arithmetic is to run with all your might. My back yard has some spotlights that lighten up most of the back yard. I will go out after a full day and sprint back and forth as fast as I can. When I come in my Dad will ask me what I was doing because he can see my cheeks are red and I'm out of breath. I will take each run and time it to myself by counting one one thousand and then two-one thousand and so on until I get to the finish line. I can tell when I'm making progress and when I need to pick it up a notch or two. I smile to myself as I break personal records and improve on my running. Those are perfect evenings to me. I always felt even when I was a child growing up. That, I feel cheated! When I do not get a chance to run and play each and everyday. I believe every person even my Mom and Dad and my sister Hannah needs to run and play. Maybe even twice a day! I'm always happy after a great day outside enjoying

The awesome sunshine and the perfect breezes God gives each of us. Days are not to be taken for granted. We need to live each day on purpose. When you live one single day so complete that it becomes a total memory you will get what I am talking about. We all have had a day or two where you can't believe the number of fun things you were able to do in one day that it seems to leave you speechless and amazed. I totally remember a day like that. It seemed surprisingly simple how it all unfolded to me. What a perfect summer morning. The temperature must have been in the seventies already.

The day started with Dad and me working on pitching together at the local school, which had a baseball diamond and a backstop. We called my friend Matt to come with us and picked him up at eight in the morning. I could tell Matt was excited too. He came running outside with his baseball glove and his baseball bat and jumped in the back seat and fastened his seat belt. We were talking all the way over to the school baseball park and laughing about what position each of us wanted to play and how many hits we would achieve that day as well. My Dad pulled in the parking lot and we all three jumped out were running for the baseball diamond to see what our talent would unfold today.

When we got there we had to catch our breath a minute. Matt yelled out, "I want to bat first." Andrew shouted," I will pitch to you." My Dad headed out for the outfield. He set himself out some where between right field and center and was hoping Matt wouldn't hit it towards left field. Even though, it would probably happen sometime that morning.

My first couple pitches were low and away. My next one was high and tight. Matt hollered out for a good pitch, which I gave him and he creamed it over my Dads head. I loved to see him running the opposite direction and totally miss judge our talent. Matt was running with all his might and hit a home run of me. I reminded him that was a gift. Matt said, "Oh no, it counts I smashed that ball." Dad threw the ball into me and I cut it off at the pitchers mound because Matt already made it into to home and was safe. We switched off pitching and batting every ten hits. By then you were usually ready to change positions. With the exception, of my Dad, he continued to play in the outfield and promised to throw the ball into home before we could get there. Sometimes he did beat us to home and we would have to back track to third base. Then we could imaginary man on third. You know what I'm talking about. We can then hit the imaginary man at third in for an easy run! Oh, yeah! Dad was so cool about the whole free run thing. It's like he had the same rules when he was growing up in the sixties. I don't mean to date everything but that is when he was a child. Hard to believe, huh!

This game was becoming crucial to me. Matt was up by three runs which were all scored by just him. He was having a field day and I was about to end his streak now. Matt seemed to be throwing pretty nice pitches up to this point. I forgot you were batter and catcher because we had only four baseballs we were working with. Still, it beat sitting at home and doing nothing at all. I was able to hone up on my baseball skills before are real practice with our new coach. Coach seemed to encourage that any way. Matt pitched one just a little below my belt, which I popped up just over second base and just in front of my Dad. He came running in and held me to a single at that at bat. So, I ran back to

Home. I got ready for my next swing. Matt threw a perfect strike, which I drove to center and I had my Dad really running hard to try and get me out. We all know that didn't happen by a long shot. I had two runs in. So now, the score was Matt three Andrew two and I had to find the perfect spot to hit where my Dad would have to run and I could get another score. Matt pitched the next ball a little low and to the right. I drove it just past his glove to the left for a perfect double and my Dad threw the ball into Matt to hold me at second. The next two pitches were too high and I ignored them and challenged Matt to get the ball over the plate. Matt said. "What plate?" Matt knew what I was talking about and got ready to throw his next pitch. He got set with his glove and decided to throw his fastball. I drove the ball over my Dads head just to the right and off he went again. I rounded first, I stepped on second, Hit third cleanly and was ready to slide into home where Matt was waiting for the throw which went to far to the right and I was safe at home. I jumped and Matt grabbed me and tried to knock my new hat off. I held on tight and laughed out loud. Matt was laughing too. My Dad came in and we grabbed our Baseball bats, gloves and baseballs and headed back to the car. What a great morning we had together. Matt had to be home by eleven o'clock. So we jumped back into the car and dropped Matt off and he thanked us. We headed home for a great lunch and some special surprises in the afternoon.

The afternoon we went to our Palatine Water Park and we ordered some lunch by the poolside and hit the water slides and swam under water with our goggles. Dad, Mom, Hannah and I swam in the deep end. Occasionally Hannah and I would swim under water with our goggles. Later that evening, we made some popcorn and watched a movie to close the night out. Those are best of the spring days to me outside of baseball. Baseball season hasn't quite kicked in yet with all the games and practices. I saw the schedule and I'm still trying to figure out which teams my friends are playing on. I know Matt is on the Indians. Well I grabbed one of my baseball books and headed up to bed. What a great day I had today. It sure seemed simple but that's what I loved about it! I was humming to myself and taking in another story about baseball.

Chapter Three
Rotating Positions

One of the first questions the coaches ask you year after year after year, is what positions do you like to play? In away it's kind of cool. You get a chance to change your mind and learn another position. Maybe I'll be a starting pitcher this year. You just hope your talent catches up with this year's new dream. It was quite funny that ten other boys had the same idea. The coaches had their way of giving all, the boy's a chance and whittling his pitchers down to this year's rotation. I made the cut! I had enough good pitches to strike out the side. I believe I can pitch in some games and start to learn what it takes down the road to pitch in more than two games.

 I always remember tossing my first little league hardball up in the air. There is just something about grasping that ball in your hand and the feel of the laces between your fingers. Half of the fun in revolving and spinning the ball in one hand, is you can show your friends some neat tricks. We all love sharing how we hold a two seam, four seam fastballs, and change up and the dreaded shhh- curve ball. Don't even mention the slider. Unless, you want to catch some well deserved trouble, from your current coach. The only truth I can cling to is how great that little league feels in your hand. We all learn to use our glove to hide the ball to master the only three pitches we are aloud to use. Mastering the fine balance of which pitch would throw off your current batter you're facing that inning. The key is putting in the change up within your rotation at the precise time when the batter is expecting a fastball. Sometime just a simple lean forward with a good mean face can look like it has fastball written all over it. That's when I like to throw my change up in. Nothing is half as funny when a batter is trying to rip at the ball with all his might only to see he totally missed the ball all together. You hear the fatal death cry from the visiting fans. Nice try honey! What the heck was that Mom thinking about, when she said that? With out a doubt I believe the roll of her son's eyes speaks volumes. Everyone knows the mom's only job is the drink and the snack. The truth is we love them there! You know mom, just keep it down a little when you are cheering. Here is how I position my fingers to throw my three pitches and juggling which pitch I will throw you next. I seem to roll the ball around in my fingers while I am searching for the seam of the ball, to get the proper fit to release the ball accurately. Its way beyond the grip you see. You have to know the fit and the release. Some how in all of this you have to keep focus on where you're delivering the ball. I like to call the little league balls final destination. I have to have a blue print for setting up my stance. The first thing I learned was the lock and ready position at the mound. The second is reaching way back as far as I can go and throwing the ball over hand toward the catcher's mitt in the strike zone. The third and final step is releasing the ball to accomplish speed (fastball) or deceptive speed (change up) to stay ahead of the batter in the count. Strikes that get by the batter will win every time and send them back to the dugout. Everything else seems to fall in place when you find your comfort spot with the fit of your fingers around the baseball. I like to do that either behind my back or within my glove. We won't even get into the mental part of pitching because I'm only nine. I'm simply not even thinking about it or Am I. Well here's the low

down on how to throw the Low down on
how to throw the two-seam fastball or
the sinkerball. Speed in the major
leagues is between 89-91 miles per
hour. For the two-seamer, the first and
second fingers lay across the narrow
area between the two horse-shaped
seam outlines. The ball is coming off the
first two fingers from four to ten o'clock
on a clock face. That causes the ball to
sink to some degree. The ball is thrown
at full velocity. The batter will only see
one pair or horizontal seams spinning,
instead of two seams spinning. The
pitch is a little harder for me to locate but
I can still throw it with good control.
The four-seam fastball is still thrown in
the major league at 89-91 mph. This
pitch is known as the heater or smoke. It
will rotate from top to bottom at 6-10
o'clock on the clock face. The batter will
see four parallel seams spinning toward
him.
The change-up (off speed pitch-fish) is
thrown 7 -11 miles slower than the
fastball. The great imposter is meant to
throw off the batters timing. The arm
motion and release are the same as the
fastball but the grip is different. The
circle change is the most common grip.
The thumb and the forefinger touch to

Create a circle on the side of the ball, which sits back close to the palm. The remaining fingers are spread around the ball. The change spreads it force around the ball instead of off the two fingers like the fastball, concentrating it in the middle of the ball and taking speed off. Different variations of the change-up are the palm ball where the ball is held in the palm and the fingers are spread evenly across the ball without the thumb and forefinger circle grip.

Well, know you know almost everything you need to know that I learned. Accept one thing. Don't ever quit or even show the batters you've had it. Just keep pressing on and work on the next batter and with a little luck and some great team mate play you will be out of the inning and thinking about batting and which pitch you want to take for a ride.

I always remember my first call. I had a main purpose that I set forth to accomplish at the beginning of the season. Mine were simple. I wanted to play second base, out field and pitch. Secondly, I want to be a more consistent hitter this year. I believe if you choose to do it, you will. So, just go out there and do it and you will have no regrets. Just give it your best even when all the elements are pounding you in the face. Whether, the sun is directly in your eyes, The rain is messing with your fit on the ball with your fingers, the cold will not allow your hands to warm up no matter how hard you blow heat from your mouth or the wind is blowing dust in your eye's. Just give it your best and you will come through on top win or lose.

My first love is second base. I feel so at home there. The drill is always the same. The coach is trying to hit a grounder below your legs and out of reach, a line drive just over your head or a mistaken pop up that he definitely doesn't want you to make the easy catch on. The other commitment you have is to defy the coach no matter what it takes. Grab the ball out of the dirt and throw it two first to get the batter out or second to get the runner out on a force or maybe third or home as well. Let me tell you what a thrill it is to catch the line drive out of no where and stop the batter dead in his tracks. Nothing will knock the batter down for the day better than a line drive catch. They are almost in disbelief. I know myself, it has happened to me. When you make the catch it is almost as if you're not sure in pure reaction time how you caught it when you did.

Make the routine easy pop-up catch and the fans will cheer every time and the batter won't. He will probably throw his Bat down in disgust. I have come to love the ready position. I need to focus harder than most guys just because I do. The outfield is a totally different gig. You really have to be on your toes all the time. There is nothing worse than running backwards after the ball and all you can here is the fans cheering and some how you have to catch up to the ball and get it back in to your cut off man who will then throw to the next base the batter is heading for to try and stop the pain. You have to make judgments with the wind and line yourself up to catch the fly or the one or two bounce in front of your play. Fielders will have to join together and one may call the other one off to make the play. But, you still have to back him up in case for some reason he doesn't make the play. You have to! I see more and more every day, it is those plays that really bond a team together to become an invincible team that won't give up and eventually win the game. Rotating baseball positions brings more depth to your skills and knowledge to make the play and take advantage of the other team. You will see Chances to take control of the game and literally catapult your team to victory. Give them the courage to come back when all things seemed like loss. There is no better feeling than the encouragement you receive for seeing the opening and seizing the moment. That is what makes singles into doubles; doubles into triples and triples into home runs! So, keep your eyes open and listen to the coach and observe what is happening when the play goes down. No place, to go with the ball. Work on timing with your teammates. Just those mundane throws back in forth-in practice give you the edge in games. You need to switch off with different players. Some have a tendency to throw high, some low and some right on. Yet, you will be able to figure out in the game situation what to do just because you have in practice. I believe the best practices are when I have learned to communicate on the field with my teammates to make the play. Believe me its not always vocal. Most of the time, it is a nod of the head, a smile or a cough. Those little tips can get you out of an inning so fast. That is baseball at its best. You usually feel a slap on the back on the way back to bat.

Chapter 4
Finding Second Base

What is it about second base? You have to be on your toes at all times. The ball sees a lot of action off the aluminum baseball bats right there. Shots, between first baseman and the second baseman. Also, between the short stop and second. The dreaded bouncing baseball grounders, to snuff up in your baseball mitt. Smashing long drives that magically stick in the baseball glove or you have to hop up to catch. The famous pop flies that never seem to come down and you have to be patient to catch. The soft throws to shortstop to turn the exciting double plays. The second baseman's terrific; throw to third to throw out the man trying to steal third base. The easy look which is thrown to first for the easy out. People only knew how awkward that throw is to make off your right back heel. The best throw which is the man at third trying to steel home plate and you nail the perfect throw to our catcher to make the tag to get the man out. You need to make the cut off throws and the short stop runs half way out to take the throw from the left fielder and the second baseman takes the cut off from the right fielder.

Second base needs to always be in the ready position. You must set yourself in a knees bent position with glove hand and throwing hand open to catch the baseball when it comes to you.
Second base is where I call home. That is my neatly fit glove position. I know where I am at I know what to do to react and make the correct play at the correct time. You see, in my mind the whole baseball field balances when I play where I belong. I have learned to play second base at the best of my ability to help our team win games. Practice seems to be the proving ground because our coach will purposely try to hit the ball through you or past you to see if you will choke. You have to believe me; I try with all my heart to make the play for I want him to think that I will make the play when the time comes. When you do and you do. There is such exhilaration that floods your soul that you can't help but smile inside and know what you just accomplished. Baseball to me is about becoming a well-rounded player that balances with his teammates to win each game. I guess that would be our mission statement if we had one. So, instead I will just make it mine for a lifetime. I

Crave for success and the thrills in accomplishments it bring along life's path. I have come to know the meaning of the phrase "I need to live my life on purpose." I begin each day with a thank you to my Lord who brings purpose and meaning to my life at home and on the baseball field. When I pray at night I will often bring to the Lord request about my baseball games. I knew from a small child God cares about each and every care of my heart. Lord thank-you for a beautiful game that I can share with my teammates (friends) and give us a year that will be full and complete. God has given me two parents whom I cherish. I have one wonderful sister who laughs, plays, reads, fights and cares for me to the bottom of my soul. My Dad, Steven often reminds me to love and care for her my entire life and she will bless me ten fold. I love Hannah with all my heart and I give her lots of hugs. Joy surrounds my house and my life. I can't always put my finger on it but it's a lot like your first dip in a cool lake early in June before the sun has a chance to warm up the water. The rippling water is so refreshing and it wakes your soul and charges your spirit from the top to the bottom.

Chapter 5
Facing The Pitcher

It seemed like just another Tuesday afternoon with just a little more on my plate today- a baseball game. Oh, Yea! The bad part is the constant reminders to finish your home work early because you have a game tonight and you will have to jump in bed right away when you get home because you have school tomorrow. I do have the baseball day routine down. I haven't missed a game yet. So, what gives! I always need a break right after school before I begin my homework. You all representing my family should have that figured out by now. Like Dad says, you only have so much creativity everyday to use. The Lord knows I'm way past that now. I'm definitely in give me a break already; I need to catch my breath mode. Get it! Got it! Good! I like to shut my door and leave the world behind and crash in my half moon chair and play Game Cube, lie on the floor and read a Matt Christopher Sports Book or SI Kids magazine. You can hear Mom hollering have you practiced your trumpet yet? Let's just throw that in front of me while I'm trying to decompress from an already extremely full day. I ending up yelling, "I know." Which seems silly to me, because we all know, I know. You, know! It was cool to read about Ken Griffey Jr. and see what he accomplished last year and what they were expecting him to do this year. SI Kids rocks!

Well, I'm getting all the baseball paraphernalia on the pants, long socks, the "you know", stretch belt which is a total pain, baseball cap and the baseball cleats. Something's up with the laces too. They seem to shrink! It has come to be a real challenge to make a bow like your suppose to tie the shoe's. Once I'm done, I'm happy and ready to go. We can all tell when he's happy in the family when we hear him humming.

Dad's always good to get some sports drinks iced in the cooler and throw my baseball bag into the car which holds my bats, batting glove, baseballs and fielding glove. I'm a right-handed fielder and batter. I don't buy into the lefty mystique. I believe you just take your natural talent and add one hundred and ten percent to it and practice. I'm just learning to develop my own practice routine outside of little league. I have learned to stretch my body. I run as fast as I can. I practice swinging my bat and driving the ball into the practice tent. The key is to bring the bat to the ball with speed. I want the opposing pitcher to think twice about what type of batter I am on the very first swing. It is extremely important he fears my swing and sees my will win attitude on the very first swing. I only know one thing for certain! I will drive that ball and you will not forget me. About the only thing and opposing pitcher can do is bean me and give me a walk. Be sure of one thing! Next time up at bat you're going to see what ball looks like when it goes to the outfield and I get on first base or better. I will not be denied. I sure love to play second base! I love to swing my bat even more. Some pitchers like to sucker me in with a change up! After, they throw me a fastball. The change up is their pitch and you feel like the ball will never cross the home plate every time they let go of the ball. What gives? Everyone on the entire planet knows that two-seam fastball is the first pitch you learn. Then the four-seam fastball is the next pitch you learn. Finally, the change up is the last pitch you learn. So, don't bother pitching change up, change up, change up, change up. You mess up our bat speed

And timing for sure! Every batter on my team will complain about you and cut you down for doing so. So, what is the point of doing so! Huh? The only thing that can make it worse is the umpire who is calling the strike in an obnoxious tone after we swung three times and missed. Every ball player's favorite pitcher gives him at least two good fastballs to belt into the outfield. The only other worse pitcher is the guy who has a funny delivery! One prime example is the one who sets up in the squat position, takes a step back and throws the ball. Are you pitching or planning on going to the bathroom. Who in the world taught you that? Have you ever seen that in the major league or minor league pitch like that? Come on! The guy who Is purposely swings his whole arm and leg behind him in attempt to hide what pitch is coming. You are not a good pitcher either. I don't expect you to broadcast your pitch. I do want a fair chance when you're throwing a fastball to have a clue what I need to do to get a good swing and drive the ball past you! You bring your best and I in turn bring my best. That's the way baseball should be. Any base runner can yell I got it when he's passing the short stop to try

To get him to move a side and watch the ball hit the ground untouched as you slide into third and you're safe. What a man! We all know kicking dust on the umpire's feet doesn't motivate your team to win. Winning is in side of you! Baseball is all about the right timing. A base hit and a man on first mean nothing when the next three batters strike out! But, a base hit and a man on first means everything when the next three batters get hits and runs score. I know there is a learning curve to pitching I have experienced it myself. You have to have all three pitches and a basic delivery to be successful at any level. I guess that is the best the other team has to give with Dad's who are first time coaches and kids who want to pitch and don't get the proper instructions on how to hold the ball and how to deliver the ball. I will just have to cope and figure out the best way to successfully get strong hits past the infield and into the outfield. I love to practice swing and get prepared to hit. I judge the pitchers timing with the previous batter and work on my bat speed coming to the plate and my step toward the pitcher. My coaches are always really hung up on that part of my batting. It's a good thing I'm not. I

Listen to their instruction when they give it. Just don't throw it in my face every time I come up to bat. We all know who the best pitchers in park district ball are. A few of the guys are Danny Haze, Vince Proterra, Codie Bobbit, Lucas Malambry and others. You have to get past the speed coming at you and get into the speed coming back at them. It truly is a battle of speed and one will win over the other one you can count on it. I have no problem with bring speed with my bat. I do have problems with my success at connecting with the ball. My success rate is about fifty percent of the time. About three years later I was fitted for contacts and that made a big difference in my seeing the ball and connecting about seventy-five percent of the time. I only delayed some great hits because of my sight. I didn't believe it was affecting my swing at all. Even still I had quite a nice year against opposing pitchers because of... You guessed it timing! We were the timeliest bunch of boys you ever met. We found a way to win a lot of ballgames though out the year. I do not specifically remember pitchers as individuals as I'm facing them. I am zeroed in on the ball. All my efforts go into focusing on the ball when

I'm at bat or fielding the ball. That is what comes naturally to me. It is first nature when I'm one on one. When I have success that is what brought me there. I guess if you know what makes you tick, you will find great moments along the way. I guess between being beaned by the baseball quite a few times and my ability to focus I have no fear when I'm up at bat. I have had singles, doubles, walks and some strike outs this year. I like to keep the strike outs to one a game if possible. You are lucky to get up to bat twice let alone three times on a school night. Our Games all have two-hour limits. I love to steal the bases too. I have had a few close calls getting back to first. The other thing I'm fortunate to have is pretty good running speed. I'm pretty good at getting a jump on the pitcher and getting on second before the throw comes and if the throw comes. Catchers like throwing that fake throw like they are going to throw you out. Only once in a while they actually release the ball and get it there for a close play. Third Base is almost a given. Home plate usually requires help from a teammate or catching everyone off guard; it will take the courage to win! Pitchers come in all shapes and sizes.

A few of them are tall. Some are short. Some are really robust. Some pitch with their right hand and others with their left. I believe for the most part you have to give them some basic respect. You just have to take it pitch by pitch to find the ball you want to clobber. I believe the most predictable pitcher is the side arm pitcher. We all know his length of throwing will be decreased from wear and tear on the arm. The pitch isn't consistent enough to hit the strike zone with any regularity. Not to mention a batters dream you can see the ball coming and it is typically low enough to meet up with your swing. Very few guys have figured out the fastball and the only time you really see them is right before they hit you some where on your body and you get your base free. I believe pitchers at this level are not going to make or break the game for you. I believe the more pitchers you have on your squad the more looks you have over your competition. Just, teach us the three pitches we need, how to reach back and throw, how to release the ball and step forward with your leg and the set position and the wind up. Pitching can be fun and shouldn't be held for just the coaches sons. Look for that hidden talent on your team. It may be the quiet kid that listens and has a ton of courage to muster up when you need it the most. I know you will feel better keeping everyone involved in baseball fundamentals. Your kids are more rounded and prepared when they have played every position and know how to play every position. They should learn it in practice so when it is game time they can apply their knowledge toward a team effort and win the game. Sometimes ask the kids to repeat back what they are suppose to do and you will be surprised how they will apply it towards winning the game.

Chapter 6
Developing My Swing

My swing shows courage, strength and quality when you see it in action. When you walk up to home plate I set the stage for my swing. I always walk up with confidence and knowledge of the pitches I like to take advantage of to win the game. Strikes and balls are one thing when the umpire is calling them. I like to be in charge of the whole experience and not fall behind in the pitch count. When you do fall behind in the pitch count it isn't over until the fat man sings. Most of the umpires in our league are men. As I weed through the selection the pitcher is currently giving me I hone in on the game breaker in hopes to win the game or get us on the way to scoring a run. The swing starts with the stance. I have a right hand swing so I begin my swing on the left side of home plate. My left front foot is parallel with right front cornet of the plate. The end of my bat should be able to touch the back far corner of home plate. I have learned a three-step swing, which we heard the high school baseball coach insists all his baseball players will do to be successful. So, if it works for them I better use it now rather than relearn it at a later date. The first step is the trigger in which you bring your left knee up slightly in my case because I'm a right-hander. The second step is you bring your bat back and slightly lowered in a set position. The third is the release where you bring the bat through all the way around. The key is your eye is beamed in on the ball and you want the ball to hit the top 2/3 of the bat. Once you run through the exercise a few times you get the swing of it. Pardon my bad sense of humor. Just remember trigger, bring your bat slightly down and swing through and hit the ball on the top 2/3 of the bat, you will develop a sweet swing as I hear the Dad's always say. I have noticed I'm even more successful at hitting the ball. I feel the new swing is comfortable and natural to do. Sixty percent of the boys that try out for High School baseball will make it. So, I have to keep my edge of hitting high percentage hits and be the first one to beat the throw at first as much as possible. Just give a 110% or more. When baseball is your class a three-hour session of practice doesn't get much better. I wouldn't trade it for Biology any day of the week. I believe

You have to keep it fun! Which isn't to hard when you have so many personalities that make up a baseball team. My swings currently add up to singles and doubles when I'm on my game. I rather be accurate than tell you differently. I'm not opposed to triples and home runs, they just haven't happened in my career at this point, yet. I have probably experienced this at least a hundred times in game time situations. Nothing prepares you for getting beaned by the pitcher ever. My first hit I took was directly in the middle of my back. I have been hit in the ankles, elbow, and shoulder at least twice a year on an average for me. You get up and shake it off, period and you have to find yourself in there and get over to first in hope to steal second or more to even the score. It definitely stings and if you're lucky you will not have any after shocks after the game. Hopefully, you will get just a little ice to take down the swelling. Get over it and approach the plate every time with the mind-set like I do that you are going to hit the ball as hard as you possibly can to get on base and set your self up for a scoring position. Baseball has to be the most important thing in your day when you are there. Even when your team is losing you can come back to win the game. I know! I have seen it first hand. We have battled back from 6-0 deficits to take command of the game and win it once and for all. You have to look deep within yourself to muster up the difference of what was missing previously and connect to win. You have to connect with yourself first. Can you visualize the hit and burn rubber to first and make sure you beat the throw and not visa versa. You have to connect with your teammates. In almost every game I can remember it is the guy you wouldn't figure to bring the first momentum to accelerate to win the game. He's usually about four feet tall and maybe ninety pounds. He looks like he is going to deliver the appropriate hit each and every time at bat. He has the beat up batting helmet on that every boy shares on the team. He has his own bat that his Mom and Dad bought at the local sporting goods store. He seems to step up to the plate with courage each time he comes to bat. You can truly see it in his stance and the brave face, which is at the very heart of him. His baseball uniform appears to be a little big on him. He's forever tugging at his pants leg to pull it up almost before every swing if the pitcher allows him to. His batting gloves are black and his two hands are gripping tightly to the bat preparing to trigger, drop down his back and swing all the way through after the pitcher releases the baseball. He truly treasures every at bat. I only can recall one time he ever walked away from an at bat. He was spitting almost incisively every time you looked at him. It wasn't like he was going to have or something. He just didn't feel good and his mother took him home with his sister. His Dad stayed to report on the results of the game. All in all this wasn't one of those rare times. You had the feeling something great was about to take place. You could hear Zack leaning on the dugout fence, "Come on Andrew!" Giving him a quick cheer to womp on the ball. Andrew kicked into his batting routine and was fully aware of the ball. He had a good visual of the seams of the baseball and could almost sense a hit was coming. Ripping the baseball is the one and only singular thought on his mind. His swing was certainly sweet enough and the bat couldn't have been positioned any better. That sound! That unmistakable sound! The sudden crack of the bat, distilling the pitch and sending the velocity of the baseball the reverse direction. The crowd roared and Andrew took off for first base with everything he had inside of him. The ball went between the shortstop and the third baseman. Neither player had a chance to make a play. Andrew rounded first and was into second base with a stand up double. He was catching his breath and adjusting you guessed it. His slightly oversized baseball pants and pulling them up again! He looked at the third base coach and was preparing to finish the ride. No sense in going just half way. It's everything to get a big hit but it's icing on the cake to pass home plate and score too! He felt calm in the midst of the confusion he created. That is totally amazing to me. Everyday at home, school and baseball is typically con fusion. When you live each day in a somewhat chaotic world. He can find success to reach his goal and provide even more confidence for his next at bat. So, Andrew looked toward the home plate and felt almost certain to score his first run today. He knew who was due up at bat after him. Evan Schaefer was a great lefty and had an unusual amount of shots down the first base line, which left the first baseman shrugged in dismay. Evan came to bat and stepped into the batters box and started his bat movement rolling round and round to prepare to meet the baseball. The pitcher releases the ball and Andrew took an aggressive lead and Evan took a full swing and hit the ball right over the second baseman's head who leaped up but not enough to make the play. Andrew reached third and the third base coach was waving him into home where he scored standing up with no play at home. Andrew nodded to Evan in a gesture of thanks and ran for the dugout with his perched bashful mouth and his teammates hit him on the helmet back and high five's him for his efforts. We realize as parents the confidence that brings to Andrew that means more to him than anything we could ever offer to him. Andrew looked toward us and smiled and we smiled back as well. The Diamond Backs were on a roll and the inning just began. No outs and Evan certainly had the same goal Andrew just had to run across home plate too. Zack came up to bat and he put another hit on the third pitch to just left of center to bring Evan around third and on his way home to score and Zack went into third safe before the throw that came in behind him. The inning seemed like it would go on forever. That's exactly how a little encouragement can snowball into runs to win the game. Andrew could be heard cheering Zack on to score as well. Zack is a pretty good player himself and gets on base about seventy percent of the time. He wrestles with striking out. They kill him and absolutely drive him wild. Zack was positioning himself for a different result. Sam came out to bat and swung at the first pitch and went to the fielder who made the catch. Zack took off from third base for an easy score. The Diamond Backs scored four more runs before they made their last out and took the lead. In moments just like that courage can lead you to succeed and build up the confidence for the next game. That's the beautiful thing about the beginning of the season. There are a lot of next games just ahead. You feel like the season will go on forever. That is a great feeling. I really feel like I'm getting the swing of this game and it has the best of me. I'm sold out! I eat, sleep, dream and play baseball everyday! I swing that bat baby with all might and every chance I get. I can see the ball coming in and I love the sound that

sends me ripping into first base to beat
the throw one more time.

Chapter 7
Batting Cage

Last year Coach Prottera and Coach Hayes worked with us in their batting cage at their home. Yes, that is right! They set up four stations for us to work at as a team. It was so very cool. The first station was for inside pitches. The next station was for outside pitches. The next station was for bunting. The last one was around the corner and was full straight on pitch. The final station you guessed it was Coach Hayes straight on in the batting cage come straight at you with his best stuff. Believe it or not only five guys showed including Vince Prottera and Danny Hayes who were the coaches sons. I was still new to the group most the boys knew each other from their church and school St. Theresa. Which was cool. I never felt out of place at all. I always felt apart of the team. My Dad stayed and helped out at the inside pitch station. I started with him at the inside pitch and started to swing and get the hang of hitting the ball when you are getting jammed inside. We took about twenty-five pitches at each station. It took Dad and I a couple of throws to get the rhythm and get the pattern down of him tossing the ball to jam me inside and I would hit the ball as best as I could into the net. Dad was doing pretty well at getting the ball in the right spot.

I moved to the outside pitch station and took about twenty swings across the out side corner. I was struggling with that a bit from where I line my self up at home plate. I have never been one to crowd the plate and so, my bat doesn't always look like it covers the entire plate when I swing. I love working on bunting because every coach has a little different take on how it should begin. It seems to be one of the best kept secrets even in the major leagues. I put the best of all I had been taught and applied it to my next twenty-bunt attempts at the plate. We worked on straight ahead pitching which was fun because I love to hear the crack of the bat when the ball comes down the middle.

My turn came with coach Hayes in the batting cage. I picked up on one thing for sure. Coach Hayes always held the ball up and gave you a good look at it before he let the pitch go. He threw, a lot of good fastballs across the plate. I sent a couple back to him in a hurry in which he snagged in his glove. It took a little while to get use to the tight quarters and feel at home in there. Especially when coach was hurling the balls in their with some pretty good speed. But, before you know it your time is up and he went through the entire bucket of balls. We learned more about hitting in one night from Coach Hayes and Coach Proterra than I did from previous baseball coaches in little league.

My Dad has taken me to batting cages outside in Mount Prospect where the machines hurl these rubber balls at you and seem in accurate at best. I always give my best and try to keep in mind they aren't very accurate. I can remember a lot of balls coming in high and tight. No matter how set you are it's hard to get the rhythm down of those funky machines. I seem to hit more grounders than line drives there. Dad was pretty good at giving me another chance and judging my frustration level with the batting machines. Batting cage work is fun for the most part. It still doesn't simulate real game situations. Like where infielders are positioning themselves. Where the outfielders have set themselves up. What the weather brings when you are up at the plate. Is the sun, pounding down on you, as it sets in front of the field? The wind seems to be blowing dust in your eyes. Not to mention what the pitcher is throwing and whether it looks prime for the taking or feels like it will never cross the plate or maybe he blew it by you and it seems like you don't have a chance. No matter what I love batting the most. It is my chance to shine and show my courage and strength. No one can give you that love for batting. It is just inside you or it isn't. Have you ever seen the boy who looks like he can't wait to get out of the batters box? He can't help it. He just isn't comfortable there. You can always here the coach encouraging (cajoling) him to take a good swing. Unless the boy is lucky, it is just not going to happen. We have all had our share of strikeouts. My goal is to have more hits than strike outs every season. The next at bat is always your chance to shine no matter what the other tem perceives of your hitting skills. I like to surprise them with my size and over power them with my deceptive strength. Andrew Sutherland brings a whole lot of character every time he comes up to the plate; I'm thinking to my self I have to get on base. The baseball field seems so open every time I look out there. So much of hitting seems to be timing and taking the pitch that looks best to you. Believe me, sometimes you only get one good look at the pitch. Your only chance to rip a good hit is your only chance. I may swing at the first pitch to take advantage of the best pitch I have seen all day. I don't smile at all. I take the whole thing very seriously. About the only thing that might upset me, is the call of the umpire if his strike zone increases. I usually will take care of that at my next at bat. Baseball is cool like that. You can usually right the wrongs if you keep your head in the game. Danny Hayes was probably the best player I have ever witness do that game in and game out. He would get a totally ridiculous call and turn around the next time at bat and make the other team pay with a triple. I call it a hunger that never seems to go away. The proof is in the pudding. Don't try to tell me I'm wrong. That extra will inside of these young men will win games every time. When I bat I bring my Armour, which includes my batting helmet, my batting gloves and my baseball bat to win. We have had pretty good luck picking out my bat every year and finding more hits every season. I always take some practice swings before I get to the on deck circle.

When I'm at the on deck circle your judging just the speed of the ball with your swing. I try never to look at the pitcher only the release of the ball is all I'm concerned with. I step up to the plate with courage and focus to do my best every time. Sometimes you don't always feel good and you have to look past those feelings and muster up some new strength to supply a hit. It's pretty amazing when you do that, you seem to forget you weren't feeling so well when you came to bat. Seems like the best medicine is a hit, right! I believe having other good hitters on your team give you good examples to follow. I can learn a lot from those players as I approach my time at bat. Guys like Vince Farina, Vince Protterra, Danny Hayes, Cody Bobbett. They are spectacular to watch and yet they seem to know what I bring to the game can make or break the season as we go. I have always felt encouragement when I'm batting and facing the opposing team. Especially when they are on the bases in front of you and wanting to score a run. They seem to be there for you when every things not going your way and give you the pop on the helmet or the slap on your tail. Those are the times I can't wait to play baseball and can't wait to be a contributing part of the team. You do build a sense of trust and admiration through this whole experience we call baseball. I like to think of the batting cages as the trenches where we see what we are made of and what we remember. The habits that are second nature or need to be developed as second nature to open up the baseball field to all the possibilities of successful hitting and strength from being prepared. It seems like we spend a lot of time practicing the fundamentals of hitting. I love those times of learning and applying and finding success in practice. I know I can find success and practice I will surly find success in game situations to contribute and help our team win the game. I remember coming home from practice beat and tired. I never remember coming home from a game feeling beat and tired. Practice makes you effective when the games on the line and practice makes you feel complete and ready to win.

Chapter 8
Getting Beaned

Taking one for the team. In the big picture it makes sense. The reality of the whole point is the pitcher has lost control of the ball. Whether it was on purpose or not. You get a walk to first base. Hopefully you escaped a serious injury from the kaleidoscope pitch. I was beaned my first year in little league. Nothing prepares you for the quickness in which it happens, the pain you feel and the composure you must find to continue on in the game. The ball was released and I could see it coming at me. I turned my back into the pitch and felt it hit me in the small of the back and then my feet left me and I hit the ground right over home plate. Coach Latell came and rubbed my back and helped me stand up and sent me to first base where Coach Jim was. I played on the Houston Astros that year. I remember hearing the crowd cheer me up after I was hit. I still tried to rub my back before the first pitch came to the next batter. Then Coach Jim had me lead off as the next batter came to plate. I believe that is where my courage to win first came from. Something changed from that point on. You find within yourself the ability to move on and play the game. Hugh Jennings has the record for being hit by a pitch. He was hit 287 times between 1891-1903. He was the first man hit by a pitch in 1887 where the official rule 6.08b a batter becomes a base runner and is awarded first base when he or his equipment (except for his bat) is touched by a pitched ball outside the strike zone, and he attempts to avoid it (or had no opportunity to avoid it) and he didn't swing at the pitch. Craig Bigio has the next closest hits by a pitch at 285 times. Walter Johnson has the hall of fame record for the most hit batsman. Inside pitching is where it all begins. Some times known as the brush back pitches. Can be ordered by the team manager and it is called plunking the ball. If the umpire determines it was done intentionally the result can be immediate ejection of the pitcher in the game. In little league the pitcher will lose his chance to pitch when he hits three batters within two innings.

On Monday April 21, 2003, Sammy Sosa had the greatest scare of his life! I was watching and was as if time stood still again! Solomon Torres a fellow Dominican Republic and a Pittsburgh

Pirate baseball player hit Sammy Sosa's helmet and broke it in half in the fourth inning. Sammy clutched his head and squeezed it. He never did hit the ground after the pitch cracked his helmet in half, which says something for his strength. Sammy was shook up from that pitch for a long time and his hits and homers ceased for a while as he gained his courage back and shook the fear out of him. This all happened not far after Sammy tied for 17th place with Eddie Murray for 504 homers. Even Sammy's own coach Dusty Baker was shocked that he didn't have a concussion from the blow. It wasn't until May 3, 2001 that Sammy Sosa hit another home run. I'm not sure to this day why I shrugged off the bean ball and continued to play and score that inning. Something in the delivery and the circumstances affects each player differently. I could have been as shook up as Sammy Sosa when my feet left the ground and I fell like a ton of bricks. I found courage and a run that inning and that made the whole episode of being hit by a pitch bearable. Sometimes in life you have to dust yourself off and keep going on with life. What do I know at nine years old accept the fact that my back is going to have a red raspberry on it for a couple days or so? I always hear that parents and friends would do anything to keep that situation from happening to you ever again. But, you know what? There isn't a blasted thing you can do to be there at that moment and time but to feel the pain, rub it off and play baseball like it never even happened at all.

Sometimes there are no parallels to your favorite player to draw from. Being hit by a pitch is the most individual experience you can ever go through. It is most certainly different every time it happens and your reaction in the situation and after the situation, are mirror opposites at best. I couldn't help Sammy and he couldn't help me either. One thing for certain eventually the dust will settle and it will settle and you will move on and have a chance to make a difference in your game for finding the courage and getting around the bases to score and give your self the just reward for fighting through the pain and finding yourself more equipped from what you have learned from a single pitch. I have beaned a person my self who got up too and went to first. This time we were able to get him out and keep him from scoring.

This season was really the crux where I found my love for baseball, the team and the most improved player ball at the end of the season. I can't put my finger on one set thing that made the difference in playing baseball that year. I can tell you my confidence made a difference in how I carried myself each game until the end of the year. "Hit by a pitch!" isn't something you run around telling your friends about. Scoring is the only thing that puts one more point logged in the scorebook. Like every good coach says, "you can't have enough runs in any game." Not every guy on the team can say they scored today. Only about half the team or a little better on a good day can lay claim to putting runs across home plate. The only foundation I can compare it to be like the songwriter who composes a song in one sitting and the melody, lyrics and bridges seem to fall in place for one day and a song is written. Yea, that is it in a nutshell. You feel accomplishment from the journey and all the parts fall in place and you feel whole as a person. You just feel whole. I didn't do anything particularly amazing that day, it just seemed to happen and happen for the better. But the melody is in my head and is oh so familiar and real and it is truly my comfort and I will hum it in my own way and not miss a part for every part contributes to the whole. Any day you can pickup your baseball bat and mitt and walk away at the end of the game and feel whole is truly a day I never want to forget. I don't every want to forget! I will fight routine things in everyday life. I don't want to handle it as routine I want to make a difference, Even if it means you brush off the dust and cringe with the pain and go to first and look for the hope of the reward. Yea, the reward is the win against your opponent team. Whether we admit it or not, its that dog gone great feeling that brings a smile to your face as we are walking back to the car to go to that routine that baseball so beautifully interrupts like the wild pitch to bring meaning to life when it doesn't make sense. Bam! It happens that fast! I guess the lesson or the reality is I don't plan on trying to even coming close to Craig Biggio's record in my lifetime. It can't hurt to have his tenacity and his incredible fans that love him for getting up and trying to win the game one more time! Just one more time-until it's your last time and you leave with that great feeling one more time!

Chapter 9
My First Hit

I dreamed my first hit would make my parents holler like that! It's a total pick up of my confidence and I'm on first base catching my breath a second from hustling down the first base line. The sound is like a loud whisper in the midst of where I am supposes to run to be safe after I hit my first hit. "Nice hit Andrew!" said Coach Jim. My coaches always seem to have the right advise for where I'm at that given day! I felt good about the hit and I do love the smile on to see my parent's faces and how proud they are of me. I truly do love them. I learned today from my first hit is the element of surprise and don't judge me by my size brings to the table. So, I stand safe at first base and Coach Jim has only one goal. Get me to second. I'm glad we are seeing, eye, to eye. I can breathe and catch my breath for a second. You have to stand up good and straight to accomplish that and hope your not tasting dust from the baseball base paths. Shortly I will spread my legs and I'll be on my toes and take off for second when my next teammate has the next hit. There is no lead-offs in this age league for nine year olds. I love the sound of the bat against the ball and the quietness that follows. In my mind time freezes for a split second and tips of the dominos that fall into one another and click in perfect timing until arrive safe at first. My immediate family and a few teammates that have taken the time to invest in me early in the season will only embrace the moment. I appreciate the early commitment of those teammates to move past their comfort zone and take the time to get to know me. A lot of times it starts out with very simple questions. Like what kind of music do you like to listen too? Are you a Cubs or a Sox fan? That one is probably the best icebreaker for any boy you meet? Even, though you get a no vote to both teams. I believe the first hit and friendships seem to follow with each season. As soon as I passed home plate Jimmy Latel was their to shake my hand and encourage me when I came back to our dugout to take off my batting gloves, helmet and put my bat in the whole in the fence. I am a firm believer in baseball makes friends. No matter what town you may go to you will find this fact is true. I have personally seen with my own eyes today for the first time. I know it will stick with me each and everyday I live. The next batter was coming up from our team to hit and I leaned through the back stop and peered through the fence hole to get my best glimpse of our little but sure lefty Jimmy at bat. This guy was tough. He simply feared nothing! Nine out of ten times he always rose up to the occasion. He did it one more time. He came up with a clutch hit to score another runner for our team. Man, he is just awesome. After watching that series of events I am inclined to say, that baseball can double your friends and gel a team into and unshakeable mold. It seems to be catching on with the parents too! Baseball has an amazing parallel to friendships and visa versa. So, as I sit back and watch my teammates strive to do their best I feel so good inside I can't possibly explain it. This seems to me to be what life is all about for me. Could I possibly handle more? I can't see that I could at this point. No not for me, as of right now. This has to be as good as it gets in my mind. Those moments are so real and full of purpose they will bring strength I can draw upon at a moments notice. That is so nice to know. Please don't write it off as a boy hood moment. I can get real deep with you and tell you like it is! I would fight and holler for purpose filled times like these that matter. After all I got my first hit today. I feel great not from the hit itself, but from the fallout of friendships that follow. From what I have seen on television it seems to be true in the major league too! That's why every boy's ultimate goal is the major league! Why would you ever want to leave the support and friendships that baseball brings and enhances your life forever. I love when you're net on deck whole experience. You put your baseball helmet on. Your baseball gloves and you grab your favorite aluminum baseball bat. You walk up to the on deck circle and your taking your best cuts and showing your strength. I believe you pick up courage and strength and just knowledge of who you are and what you have accomplished up to this point. Lets face it, even if your one of the best guys on the team the coaches have know clue whether or not your going to get a solid hit, pop up, ground out or bunt. Each time you're at bat it's a matter of what you are seeing and the pitcher is giving you over home plate. People believe a lot of things with this battle. I believe the batter always has the edge over the pitcher. You always have a chance to connect with the ball and get a base hit minimum. I like to call it a three-step success system. Track it, meet it and follow through. You do have to focus and zero in on the ball and if you can see the seams of the ball you have the best chance for sure. What happens is some how you have to tune out everything around you except the pitcher. Some how visually and with what you hear you find your timing and you have to swing fast enough to meet the ball and send it where the infield and outfielders aren't positioned. Greatness comes when you achieve that and find yourself on base and in position to score. Somehow you have to slow down time enough to accomplish the basics. It's kind of like, set, step and swing. This all has to happen in that one clear moment where you can break down what the pitcher is giving you at that given time. Face it; you get as many pitches as the count allows you. Three strike and four balls are all you get. Whichever one comes first. That is plus or minus any foul balls that come after two strikes. Believe it or not we may never truly know who holds the record for consecutive fouled off pitches. They didn't track these numbers on early baseball history. A guy name Appling fouled off 24 balls against Ruffing. If that happened in little league I believe the umpires would turn red and get really mad at you. In my case you never want to get there. All though I have had some of my hardest hits at full count where I have two strikes and three balls. Something about when the games on the line and you have to come through that some how you do just that. Amazing, miraculous, incredible, fantastic, tremendous, all these words don't nail down what is happening. Except one phrase, I did it! Believe it or not that's when I like to succeed. I have gone down to and haven't been able to get ahead of the count. All you can do is come u to bat the next time and determine within yourself to do some damage and catch the other team by surprise. More likely than not that is when you make a name for yourself and people start telling other friends about your accomplishments. That is so cool and so humbling to me. I have never been good at taking compliments at all. I just can't swing with tem. I don't feel like I'm anything more than a boy who just loves to play the game of baseball. I do believe good hitters are born. From what I heard from my Mom I was swing before I hit my first baseball field. I have always been good at going after what I wanted. My Dad loves to tell the story about hiding under a blanket once and I came up and took a big chomp out of his nose with my new sharp teeth and was laughing silly about it. Believe me he wasn't. I sure got what I was after. That kind of tenacity will bring you ahead of the count rather than behind the count. If you ask me what is important? I would have to answer that very moment when you add excitement to the game with everything you bring. You are important to each and every game. I know that and that is why I bring my A game every time. I can only remember one time I felt so physically sick my mother took me home right away and I was next at bat. Yes, I must have been pretty sick because that is not like me at all to give up my bat. My Dad was speechless. He couldn't believe I felt that sick. So, he stayed so I would know later the outcome of the game because the game was very close at that point. It should be the exception not the rule if you love playing the game of baseball. A great game will be waiting for me the next time when I have my act together. My first hit was fulfilling. I believe I will always remember it. My best hits are yet to come. I want to improve and make strides to truly be better each year. I want to be the best I can be and focus through the moment and get the moment down to two people and be the one and the end of the dual that comes out on top. I can accomplish what I set out to do. Great moments are made from the moment. The moments define you. That is it! The moments define you and show who you really are. I can improve and will improve with time. Baseball will be waiting for such a time as this where moments define who I am really. God grants you the moments to see yourself clearer than use those moments and shine through them and god will surely shine through you to show his wondrous and awe inspiring works. A simple hit- no a moment made clearer.

Chapter 10
Stealing Bases

Stealing bases begins with finding that imaginary line toward second base where you have gone just about to far off first base that your close enough to second base. Stealing bases is my third love in baseball. We can all recall playing steal the bases when we were younger. I used to play with my Dad and Rob between to big trees in our front yard. Whoever was running was daring the basemen to throw the ball in a rush in hopes that they would throw the ball away. I would end up get maybe two or three bases. Baseball is a little different deal then running bases. The only variable that stays the same is your own competitive edge against the competition. The first hurdle Is judging the pitchers throw to the catcher and watching how alert the pitcher is returning to the pitchers mound. Most cases my brain would flash back to prior base running situations and the out come for the runner from our team. I could visualize our runner clearly making it safe to second base without any problems. For some crazy reason the pitcher in little league is more willing to give you second base. Unless the pitcher has a good quick move to first and I believe that would be about one third of the time. Every team has one pitcher they can truly count on to get strikes and keep guys off the base. Even then the pitcher will give away his throw to first in his set position. The head of the pitcher is cocked a bit differently and will give his move away. That is when I like to use reverse thinking and show I give up on my pursuit of second just long enough to get him focusing back on the batter instead of me and then I will make my move for second. I like to think of stealing as stealing. When your heads not in tune with what is going on that you will lose the goods. Which in this case is the next base. When you're running from second base to third base, I have only seen a pick of only two percent of the time. Most of the time in little league if you have a good amount of guys on base you can really capitalize on scoring if the other teams throw is off by inches. Baseball is a game of inches. You see it almost every week. One throw of by an inch can set the ball soaring into center field where the center fielder isn't use to seeing the ball come back to him in that situation. Sometimes the center fielder could be set for the stop and have trouble picking up the ball and then he is trying to figure out which player he has the best chance to get out and which team mate he should throw the ball too. I have seen more mistakes out behind second base than anywhere else. The only place I have ever seen good execution is in the minor league with the Schaumburg Flyers. Once we were there early enough to watch them practice throwing the ball from all positions to any other position relating to their cut off men. The rules were different for out fielders than they were for infielders and the battery. The rhythm and the precise throws were so incredible that you could see the exactness in their execution. They literally didn't miss a beat between each throw. Each player knew when the ball would arrive and kick the ball out to the next player who knew when that ball would arrive. Click, click, and click. Talk about knowing your other teammate to the T they really did. The sound of the pop of the ball in the mitt was like when you and your Dad played ten feet away from each other. I promise you they couldn't have been any farther away from each other and it was as if they were ten feet away. Amazing, simply amazing. I believe that is how our team should warm up more than the pitcher with the catcher, the first, second and third basemen trio. The left, center and right fielder throws. We should all get in our positions and practice like the flyers did less boys would be willing to take a chance on stealing the base if they know how solid you all play as one unit. This will literally set you apart from your competition. You will freak the other team out. When you see it performed it actually if done right will send chills up and down your spine. Really! That continuity will be unstoppable by the end of the season. Your belief system is strengthened and your confidence is through the roof. No one on the planet earth will be brave enough to try anything after seeing that in practice. Practice does make perfect. Confidence does bread success. Again, this is little league where your chances double and triple. You have to love it. The throw to third is opposite of the throw to first. If, inches is on your side there is only one fielder to make the stop, which he for sure won't have a play at, third and most likely miss you at home again. You see a lot of double clutch from fielders at this age because they want to make the appropriate throw. The sight line is off compared to first not to mention the throw is shorter if he is right handed. The old right-handed pitcher and left-handed pitcher can be an advantage at first or third depending on whether you are righty or lefty. The toughest stealing is to home plate. Most of the time you will see three outs before you will see a boy brave enough and fast enough to steal home literally in front of the pitcher and catcher. Any kind of direct hit on your body will most certainly be felt. Ouch! So, which base do I love to steal? I would have to answer first would be first, second would be second, third would be third and home would be cool if I have the courage. I consider them stepping-stones that lead to the next step. It's like a single jump in checkers. Most of the times, strategy wins in checkers and in baseball. At least that is what I have found out from experience. You have to most certainly feel greatness and confidence in your very first step. It is truly imperative. You might say it is a must and builds trust. Like going to a dance, with no romance. Why even bother. No risk! No growth! That is exactly the point. I am going for second base now and I will be safe I am faster than your throw! You can't compete with that unless you are the Schaumburg Flyers of little league. I haven't seen that yet! Most of my coaches like you on the balls of your feet. They want your legs spread wide. In case you have to go back to the previous base you can make a move forward or backwards. Your hands up from your sides and ready to pull into action as you take off. Baseball seems to be a lot of lessons like this you build on from being in the situation and knowing how to react with the correct baseball knowledge enough to do the correct movement to be successful to complete the task at hand. That is why your baseball cleats must be tied before you get to the game. Who has time for all that nonsense? Every Umpire that has called time-out to tie baseball cleats has cost them a strike at bat. I promise you that. The kind where he clicks the strike on his counter so you can see it. Don't kick dust on the messenger today. Tie your shoes and be ready to fly either way. Scoring is fun! I like to score every time just for the punch in the arm from a fellow teammate when I hit the bench after running the bases successfully. I like being one of the first runs rather than the tenth run. Especially when your playing slaughter rule. You know, when a player scores the final run by a pre determined deficit that clichés the game. No one likes that guy who scores that run on either side. You may have been next to bat. Just not as rewarding, as being the guy to get the game rolling. Remember this, all runs are good. Say it with me in unison. All runs are good. I believe you have got it! Stealing bases is everything about having your head in the game. It is so much fun. You're sure to get a way to go from the first base coach or the third base coach. Way to goes are as good as they come! Coaches really get into the game when the runs start accumulating. Coach Hayes usually took first base coach and Coach Tyack took third base coach. They were like glove positions for both of those guys. They knew what to do and had their roles down. The stealing signs too. We always had a couple of those to keep the other team guessing. You can make quite a name for your self with more people than just your Mom when you show people you know what to do to score. Stealing bases creates opportunities and is the best show case for your baseball skills. That is so cool. You are clicking on all cylinders and making a difference in the game. Getting the next base is like the next reward. The side of your foot touches the side of the bag until you move side ways again with the stance and arms ready to hit the next base when the next opportunity comes up. So, be ready to have fun and be ready to fly with all guns flying and be safe at all costs. Remember I'm all about living life on purpose. I have so much fun that way. I have noticed it can be contagious too!

Chapter 11
Early Seasons

So, here we go. The start of the baseball season has come and I'm ready to make some memories with some pretty awesome boys. Nothing beats a great day at the ball diamond playing catch and cracking baseballs. I can see Coach Tyack digging the bases out of the baseball locker behind the backstop. I ran up and helped out by taking a base out to where second base should be. I knew enough to line it up with the pitchers mound and home plate. The trick is finding the pre-made hole with the rectangle pipe that the base fits on. Usually there is a rope tied to it to act as a flag to signal where it is. Every time we find our selves digging for the pipe so we can set the base on it and get on with practice before the game. Well I found it and second base is secure and was ready for some B. P. (batting practice). We have a cool rule. Who ever shows up first gets to bat first and get the coaches first rusty pitches. So, the way I see it, I will bat second and boy I am ready to hit today! Coach is walking to the mound with the big bucket of baseballs and his old baseball mitt.

His mitt looks incredibly large. Coach has on his olive green cap and is motioning his son Sam to bat and encouraging the rest of the guys to be ready. Coach seemed to be throwing hard and Sam took the first pitch a solid grounder bouncing up the third base line. Sam took every pitch to a different area through out all his B. P. today. Coach said, "Alright Andrew." I came up to bat adjusted my baseball pants quickly and adjusted the socks and I grabbed my bat and I was ready to swing. I had to get adjusted in the naturally cleat made hole by home plate. I remember it from last year and was one more thing to contend with when everyone is batting. All you can do is give your best the whole will probably never be repaired by Palatine Park District real soon. Coach through the first one high and I swung and missed. He through the next one low at the knees and I took it to right field. I believe I was swinging late because it was barely fair. The next pitch was perfect and I drove it up to the right of second on one bounce. The next pitch was inside and I drove it into left field. I have to admit coach was giving me totally different pitches every time. The last pitch was perfect and I drove it between center and right field. Then the rest of the boys went through batting practice and I took my spot at second base. I liked to get as many stops as I could because the coaches were always watching. I like to avoid being corrected n front of the guys as much as possible. Sometimes there is nothing you can do about it. The coaches are just trying to stop real quickly and give a snap shot of what we should do in that situation. I don't take it personally at all. I just rather not be the one guy singled out for the example.

The coaches from the other team were getting hyper so we ran off the field and followed our coaches to the dugout for what we like to coin our pre-game pep talk. Coach Hayes usually did the pep talk and he was good at being firm and driving the point home and what our chances were based on practice today. If we were off he would just come short of telling us we would get slaughtered. If the team looked sharp he would simply say you better wake up out there. Today it leaned toward the second pitch, high and tight. He was right and we listened to him because he knew baseball inside and out. I mean every facet of the game from the rules to fielding and running the bases and hitting. He would look you right in the eye and wouldn't cut any slack. He knew what was at stake or as I like to think what our potential could be. In the end we make or break or team. I believe these discussions push us and give us the motivation we need. We could now slam some electrolytes and get prepared for the game. I never knew if I had Gatorade or XS Sports Drink Dads house brand from his business. I didn't mind they were both good. Once in a while he would bring his XS Energy drinks and one was Rootbeer Blast. We were the home team so we were getting our baseball gloves and hats to be prepared to hit the field. The little league umpire for Palatine baseball signaled to both teams that the game was about to start. Coach Tyack just came back and went over the boundaries and other key rules that the umpire felt was important to share with us. Danny Hayes got the start for pitching today. He was our best pitcher and early in the year he was pretty much un-hittable. I knew Sam was at first, I was at second base, Cody was at shortstop and Evan at third base. I really went inning by inning and everyone sat out a couple of innings and we all played almost every position. Today our challengers were the Cubs being coached by Coach Rose and Coach Schumacher. Coach Rose was commissioner this year too! I knew Jack Shoe and Jack Rose and Dakota Adams from Pleasant Hill Elementary School. I always enjoy playing against Dakota. He was a great diver for the ball and his uniform was usually pretty dirty by the end of the game. All right, the game is on the way. Danny was throwing hard and the first pitch was a strike to Shoe. Danny second pitch was inside at hit Shoe and sent him to second. Shoe was grabbing his wrist and trying to shake it off. His Dad had his arm around him encouraging him to shake it off. I can always feel the added pressure when my buddies our on base. The key is to get them out and avoid bragging rights. Jack Rose came up and hit Danny's first pitch to our first baseman and he picked up the ball and stepped on first base and through the ball to Cody at second base and Shoe was out too. Coach Hayes was tipping his hat to the infield. Danny struck the third batter out and we were out of the inning. Coach Hayes was yelling out, "Great heads up ball guys!"

There is something about starting a game like this with three quick outs. Practically the whole team feels the boost, including the guys on the bench too! Trust is building with key plays like this. The knowledge you can be successful in working with one another. Evan was our lead off man, than Danny and then Cody. I was up after Cody today. We were surprised to see Dakota was pitching first for the Cubs. Evan come up and was whirling his bat around and stretching it behind his back and stepped into the batters box. Evan cracked the first pitch being a lefty up the third base line for an easy single. The left fielder through the ball back to Dakota and he caught the ball went back to the mound and adjusted his hat down and prepared for the next batter. Danny came up and smashed the ball over the center fielders head and we were up two nothing just like that. Dakotas cap went down a little farther. Cody came up and took the second pitch to right field for a double. I was pretty fired up and about as ready as I could be. Dakota got me to a three and two count. My strikes were one swing and one foul. Then the last pitch came in a little low and I drove to the left of the second baseman and

Cody rounded third and went to home and it was to late, Cody was safe. I made it to second for a double. The next batter from our team Zack popped up to second for an out and I stayed put. Our next batter Tim struck out just missing his last swing. Brian came up and on the first pitch hit the ball to left field and I was safe at third base. Joe was up and took the third pitch back to Dakota and I crossed home plate but Joe was out at first. We had a three run lead in the first inning. The next inning the Cubs players were three up three down. So, we really never scored the next inning leaving guys on base. Then we had to face Jack and Shoe again and they both hit doubles and the score was 3-2. We did stop them that inning delaying the pain. That is the problem with early leads you think you have clinched early. You never quit fighting. We came up to bat again and had some nice hits including a single by me. We just couldn't seem to get home to score and we were out in the field again. New pitchers were in now and both teams were holding their own. The Cubs got two men on with walks by Zack who was struggling early.

Dakota came up and hit a double scoring their two runs and taking the lead. Coach Rose and Coach Shoe were out of control with enthusiasm. We got their next batter out on strikes and Zack went back to the dug out and threw his baseball cap. Coach Tyack told him to knock it off. You know we had still had our last at wraps. Cody started us off with a single. Than. I hit a line drive that was caught at short and Cody was thrown out at first. That guy was so lucky to pull that one off. I remember Cody slapping me on the back and saying, "Nice hit kid!" I was in disbelief. No matter how we cheered on our last batter he dropped to his third strike. Amazing as our start was we lost the game. Cubs became more than just another team. Somehow we just knew the finals would come through them again. They were feeling very proud right now which they had a right too. We knew we weren't a fly by night team. We will be contending for division but we will have to focus on our next game next week. We have two games next week! No time to mope around we have to get our next game to be a win. Our coaches slapped us high fives as we came in!

Chapter 12
Pop Flies

I will always remember this as one of my favorite practices with Coach Hayes. I don't totally understand why we practiced pop flies that Monday Night. I will always remember how challenging and how much fun I had that one night. Coach Hayes had us always stretch before every practice and game. There was a routine to stretching the legs and then stretching the arms. First we put both legs in front of us in a V and reach out to touch the toes. The take you're left leg and bend it behind you and reach for the right toe. The do the same with the right leg. We stand up and put the right arm behind you're head and stretch it out and then the left arm. Coach Hayes had us all come in a huddle and he sent us for a lap around the field and he was running with us. I mean he was moving and we were all having trouble keeping up with him. The closest guy was Cody. We all finished huffing and puffing and grabbed our gloves and headed for left and center field and Coach Hayes stayed at home with his favorite bat. He started slamming balls all over the outfield and we were playing five hundred until different guys were knocked out. Each hit was very challenging. The wind was unbelievable that night. The baseball seemed to soar forever. Every know and then Coach Hayes would stop hitting and meet us half way to explain approaching the base ball with your glove and using both hands. He showed us diving for the ball plays. He perfected running backwards and making the catch behind you. We worked on this the whole night and all had about six of each style of out fielding before we left that night. I think Coach was having fun with us and sent us running, a whole lot and all over the place. I never had so much fun and felt that challenged. I felt my side aching and it didn't seem to matter until the night was over. Now The Diamond Backs were learning to face the challenges of outfield as a team. It was an extraordinary night trying to get points and learning on the way. Drops cost you to loose all your points and start all over. I didn't care I was learning and having fun along the way. Especially as the night went on I could see the twilight was playing havoc with our effectiveness and our abilities. Guys were starting to get reckless cutting each other off so Coach Hayes kept us all in check by saying this one is for Andrew, Evan, Zack, Cody and so on. He was the kind of Coach you listened too immediately.

 Boy, I never can remember a practice that just put a smile and made me laugh and I felt so good. I love to have fun and laugh my side silly and do hat with my friends, family. I do believe I'm very similar to a lot of people. We all long, to have fun and push the envelopes a little more. I liken it to coming down from the high of sugar. Great while you're enjoying it. Some things in life click and just happen. You can plan it. Like holidays where everyone going to pull out board games and you have fun and play. Sometimes just getting them started with so many individuals Is a real battle. It seems that, nine times out of ten fun times develop all on it's own. It is spontaneous. Those times become contagious and out of control. It hurts to laugh and your eyes water. Laughter rises loud enough to pierce people's ears. They seem to fly by at high velocity and leave time lacking even after a very full day. I long for those times and they make me so complete and full as a person. Growth really occurs and intimacy through those times. You are closer to complete strangers when you can break through and make the day an event. We went to meet up with some friends in Florida and played in the ocean and learned to snorkel together which I never did. We laughed and discovered treasures in the ocean and learned to walk backwards with fins on. At the end of the day we were playing tennis with no lights on the court and dusk was stealing our time together. We were invited as a family to stay past lunch into dinner and it still went to quick. My whole family enjoyed the whole day too. That is amazing to me. We had ice cream, lunch, dinner, conversations, pool time, snorkel in the ocean, saw beaches being made, watched television, played tennis, saw giant turtles, found sand dollars and made new friends. In life we learn that these times are rare and they are so important to grow and be a complete person. I don't feel complete as a person most of the time. Sometimes I'm reminded that I'm incomplete. I didn't make my self this way. God did. I'm still learning that each day I'm a new creation. I don't feel like it when I fail and I disappoint people most of the time. I have what seem like natural responses to tease and have fun to create more of those times but they tend to blow up right in front of my face. I want to make people laugh but I don't always go around the right way to do that. I can hurt people when my intentions aren't always bent that way. Sometimes I know I'm wrong and other times I'm just lost. People seem to see the same reaction from when I'm frustrated and want no part of me. Instead of, coming up beside me and being a friend. Friends stick closer than a sister, even when you tick them off. I can remember my friend Rob just leaving in the morning and later that night we were back outside making the good times happen on the Razors. After all I'm just a kid. My Dad has told me time and time again, that God has a lot of plans for my life that will blow all our minds some day. My family is in my court and loves me with all their hearts. I can see them encourage me at home. They are at very game they can make and some practices too. I have seen some talented boys on my team that ride their bikes to games and practices and I don't recall ever seeing whom their mom or dad is. So, I know I have a very supportive family. I'm not blind. I am bent though to enjoying life completely and naturally. So, however we can pray for those times to be the majority and not the minority is more in line with my hopes. I know life isn't perfect. I have recovered from losses and dreams that our crushed and bad afternoons. I believe we are the same in this cause. We want to enjoy one another and make a difference and be creative and fun. Here's to one more practice like pop up flies to make my day awesome. Anytime you can remember the passion and the hunt I believe you are in the game and you have won. So, when you look at me I pray you see the person not the problem. I hope you see the creation God made. I hope you believe and pray with all your heart that God can do anything! He helped one hundred and twenty people survive The Roman Empire. I know he will complete his work in me. He will complete his work in me! So, the night came to an end as dusk took over our pop flies field. We gathered up our baseball equipment to head home. Coach Hayes. I just want to thank you for a fun night at practice that will live strong in my baseball memories.

Chapter 13
Middle Season

Wow, the baseball season is clicking by. The Diamond Backs find themselves with more wins than losses under are belts. We have grown tighter as a team. We see the value in every player and you can tell by the surprise look at times that Coach Tyack enjoying the ride too. We have lessons to learn and have had some tough drizzle rain games we played through and won. Those were some serious character building days. I can't remember I'm wet an uncomfortable until we are heading home and I'm talking about taking a good warm shower. What a bunch of characters The Diamond Back boys are. Fun, tough, tenacious fighters that can put some runs on the board. I feel like I'm hitting better this year. I know when I come to bat I will have more success than lack of. I'm still not fond of striking out. Every boy on our team strikes out once in a while. Starting to see a difference between faster pitching and slow pitching. We all as a group have more trouble with the slower pitcher because of the timing thing. Mid season is feeling good and are momentum has come along way from the Cubs game. You learn a lot from the first game of the season. We are not playing long enough as a team to know what to expect from one another. We know that a couple runs separated us from succeeding that day. We were awful close to getting there that day. We know that as a team. We have played teams that hit much better than the Cubs do. I'm sure they will play some of these teams too. I can tell you talent and timing will take you along way. We are working on bunting at hit and run situations in practice. The team is looking sharp as a whole. Brian is hitting much stronger and Zack is out of control. Rotating positions is helping us to know where cut off throws go. Evan has become quite a good pitcher. It's that lefty advantage thing they always talk about. Us right handed player don't believe that for one minute. They just look different and throw your timing off. I believe you have to block that out and focus to find your hits. Plus the weather has improved and we are moving into those warmer Saturday games. I notice the parents are gelling and become an awesome support for us. We haven't played Mats team the Cincinnati Reds yet. I'm looking forward to that! Our pitching rotation is pretty well set and I should get a chance to try pitching for an inning or two this year. All you can hope for is a little more opportunity if you want to try a position. We have a lot of guys on this team that enjoy playing catcher. Which is nice compared to the Astro's where we had a handful and they were worked a lot even though they didn't mind it. School still adds its pressures with homework. I'm doing pretty well in all of my subjects. The best part of mid season is summer vacation is just around the corner. Baseball is the perfect fit to bridge between school and summer vacation. Time seems to mesh well with wrapping up spring-you know April, May and June. There are enough games and practice and just enough homework to push the end of school along and bring on our awesome summer vacation. Baseball has a way these days of making school bearable. I 'm not counting the days left for school when I have a team to support and catches to make and hits to deliver. The rhythm is perfect and escapes the drain that a full school day can zap out of you. School is cool for the most part. I'm finding some interests that click with who I am.

At times I can see my shadow. My shadow is the undefined part of me. When I look at it I can only see the scale of who I'm becoming. I see the height with no details. I walk my life and conform to the routine and occasionally I can see myself clear in the reflection. I like myself. Andrew's becoming is a process that is similar to that puzzle piece that blends in with the right colors and seeks for the opportunity to be the perfect fit and make the picture complete. My Grandpa Sutherland is great with puzzles. I can still see his sunlight porch and the white table where he has the latest puzzle of the week working. My Grandma Della was never bothered with the puzzle being worked on out there. It was just Grandpa's spot to hang out and find some solace there. I believe he did. I can remember joining in on the endless staring and occasionally I would place apiece right where it belonged. I was curious about this process where the picture may not be complete until the end of the week. I liked the idea that it didn't half to be completed that afternoon or before we went to sleep. The fact that you could come back to it several times a day and find accomplishment in complete the lower left corner section. My Dad has no patience for puzzles though. He would have to complete it before the day ended or it would totally drive him nuts. All three of us as a generation work at puzzles very differently. Grandpa can take a whole week to do it. I would probably take two to three weeks to do it; My Dad would have to finish it in one day. I on the other hand can come and go and work at completing the puzzle in my own time. I have been afforded the luxury of seeing the picture clearly. I may through time be able to put the pieces together and see life more clearly. School and home life is that way for me. Only, when I play baseball does the field and the hitting and the plays develop the picture instantaneously for me in such a real way. So, I admIre my Grandpa wisdom to take the time to let the puzzle become the glorious picture. I understand my Dads obsession to have the picture completed right away. I guess I see through both of them that in life you can figure out the puzzles you face quickly if you need to, or over time if time affords it. We all long for complete pictures. I know I won't have my Grandfather forever. For right now I can enjoy watching him solve a puzzle and join in at solving it with him when I choose. Sometimes two people can solve the puzzles a little faster. The sunlight room brings light on the puzzles we face in life. They help us see the puzzle a little clearer. Oh, there is another perfect fit. Amazing how you can look at a puzzle on time and never see exactly where the pieces fall. The next time they seem to fall right in place, one after another. I know my Grandpa is in that time of life where he is completing his picture. He seems to have a purpose in his walk everyday. He's touching lives right where he is. He loves to read and work by his computer. He loves to listen to all types of music. When I sit in his lap I get the overwhelming sense in my soul that he understands me and accepts me with open arms. You might say he has taken the puzzle out of my life and helped me fit right where I belong. I will forever remember Grandpa Bob for that and cherish it in my soul of souls, I thank my God for that brave man who found life through the toughest puzzles he faced in his final picture being completed. The good news is he will have a complete picture in heaven someday.

Mid season has been so enjoyable. Even through the endless hot evenings where we are sucking down our drinks and grabbing our bats for the next sequence of events in tonight's baseball game. I can see the friendships locking in on our team. You see it in, the way each boy just shares, how he feel after a play. The way they can tease one another and get under the other guys skin. The laughter you hear, from each boy that seals the win for tonight's game. The fresh cool breeze, that came out of nowhere to cool all of us off and bring relief when we needed it. The stop after the game at Mc Donald's for a shake and a burger before I hit he sack. You have to believe the mid season is picture perfect at best and is ushering in a final season that perhaps we will never forget. I'm ready for the hit the sack part and calling it a day. But, before I fall a sleep keep this fact in mind. I was made for this time and our team is preparing ourselves for some awesome dreams tonight. Some incredible dreams just a head for our seasons end. The picture will be made a little more complete and that will be sweet.

Chapter 14
Seasons End

I can hardly believe this season is wrapping up so quickly. Today is the second Monday in June and my mom reminded me that we only have two more games this week on our schedule. I can see my uniform is all ready to go in my room. I have the routine of getting all the sox's, baseball pants and Diamond Backs shirt and baseball cap on before the big game. I guess I'm excited about participating in tonight's game. I really believe in myself. I know my hitting has picked up and I can see great results in each game. I look in the mirror at the boy in the baseball uniform and I can see the confidence this game has brought me. I can just envision the baseball field and parents and teams at both dugouts. The umpire giving out the foul lines and out of bounds boundaries. I can hardly wait for tonight's game. I grab my baseball bag with all the gear. I get my drink. I put my Diamond Backs hat on and I'm ready for action. My Dad is ready to take me he grabs his car keys and we say good-bye and see you later to Mom and Hannah. I can see we have an awesome day to hurl the ball around. Today was made for baseball. Baseball was made for today. We tolerate baseball when the weather conditions are cool and rainy. Something about those seemingly perfect days that make the baseball memories even sweeter. We are heading over to Sundling Junior High to their baseball diamond behind the school. The outfield is a little rough the way I remember it. Which can make for trouble even on a beautiful day like today. The ball seems to bounce crazy and will sometimes get stuck in a rut. So, you just do your best and hope the ball bounces in your favor. We pull up to the school and I can see we arrived at the same time Coach Tyack made it their with my teammate Sam. Sam grabbed his baseball bag and one of the big team bags and headed for the Diamond. We knew today was significant. Even the other team was arriving and had a pretty serious look on their face. I can see right through that and know we are going to beat those Palatine White Sox today. I know there are always one or two kids on the team that surprise you, because I am one of them too. I could sense a win was just around the corner and we just had to play with all our might to be the victor at the end. Zack came in on his bike with a big smile on his face. I always wondered where he lived and how far he rode his bike. He had the baseball bag hanging on the handlebars of his bike and rubbing against his bike tires. You could see the tire marks on his bag. Evan came strolling up and turned his baseball cap off kilter just enough that you wouldn't take him seriously. It was a thing with Evan. Even when he warmed up he would try to fake the other team out and let them think he was a lousy pitcher to all their hopes up. Then Evan would bring out his killer pitches and let the other team have it. Cody came with his Mom and Coach Hayes arrived with Danny who was grinning with confidence too. I can't wait for the Play Ball cry from the umpire today. I could see Danny sharing his sunflower seeds with guys on the bench and watching the other team practice. The coach was hitting balls to all of his players at all their positions and they were working on cut off men. You could see their timing was off and they had a lot of drop balls and not catches. The coach was kind of hollering at them. Our coach asked for practice time about ten minutes later.

We were working on throwing with our partners. Sam and I were clicking and the throws were consistent and hard. I could see we would have good exchanges between second at first base our respective positions. Coach Tyack had us take our positions on the field and Coach Hayes swung hard hits at us. We were getting some pretty good grabs including Cody at shortstop that already managed to dive for one of Coach Hayes zingers and had dirt all over his uniform. My turn came I timed my pick up and throw to Cody and shortstop for the tag on the base and he had a great throw to first base for and out. I heard away to go from Coach Hayes how was getting ready to hit one to Sam at first base. Coach Hayes had some awesome slams to the out fielders who were running to get the ball and get the throw to the cut off men. Coach Tyack waved us in and we headed for the dugout to get ready to bat we were the home team today. We all ran to check out the line up and I was the sixth batter on our team today. I was sitting out the third inning and the sixth inning. I went and put on my batting helmet and gloves to practice my swings against the fence. My Dad would throw the ball up in the strike zone and I did a good ten swings or more. I went up to watch Evan our awesome lefty batter take his at bat. Evan again was doing the slothful batter like he was a bad hitter for the other team. He took the first pitch down the first base line for a single. It was kind of close and appeared that Evan was swinging a little late. He beat out the throw. Coach Hayes was giving him the business for not hustling. Zack came up to bat and hit a liner to their shortstop and was out. He had to blurt out his anger again and slammed his bat down when he got to the dugout. Danny Hayes came up and took the third pitch to the centerfield and scored Evan at home and he was on third base. So, a nice triple for Danny Hayes and the crowd was going nuts. It was beginning to look like I might bat this first inning. Sam had a nice single and scored Danny at home and we were up two runs and our bats seemed very hot. Brian came up and hit a hard one to the third baseman and the throw was late and Brian was safe too. I came up and the pitcher threw the first pitch, which I took. The umpire called, "Strike" at the first pitch. Coach Tyack was encouraging me to swing and get a nice hit. The second pitch was released and it was perfect and I grabbed a hold of it with my bat and for an instance time slowed down as I watched the ball accelerate off my bat and head over the right fielders head. I ran to first base and ran into second at beat the throw and I could see both Danny and Brian scoring and my parents and sister yelling from the sidelines. Wow, that was fun. I could tell the White Sox were a little upset because our first inning was rocking so well. I can't blame them I would be mad too. I knew this would be an awesome game for us because each week our hitting was getting stronger and stronger. The team was playing great as a team. Not to mention we looked cool in our Diamond Back uniforms too. We were up four runs like wild fire and had seven innings to go. They managed to get two more outs with our next batters so I ran home and hung up my bat in the chain link fence by my handle at put my gloves and batting gloves back in my bag which was hanging on the fence I grabbed my mitt and hat and headed out to second base where Cody gave me slap on the back and said, "Way to go kid!" I tried to hide my smile but it was impossible. We were starting the bottom of the first with a four run lead and Evan was getting ready to not show them his great stuff. He was amazing. I'm not sure if the other team always fell for it because usually he had one or two buddies trying to turn him in. Cody just completed a nice underhand toss to me in practice at second and I threw it to first with lightening speed with all my might To Sam who made a nice play at first with the back of his foot and a great stretch and catch. I believe more confidence comes in those warm up times when you know you are connecting out there. The innings seemed to cruise by and we scored one more run with a double by Zack, which made him happy in the third inning. So, we were up 5-0 in the third inning. Danny ended up getting a home run in the sixth inning to win the game and we all went out to Dairy Queen for ice cream after the game. I got a kick out of seeing which guy ordered what dessert for his favorite. I was sitting with Cody and Zack and were all passing the time away retelling the game and having some great times for sure. You can't beat a win, some ice creams and your teammates for some of the best of times in our final season.

Chapter 15
The Play Offs

We all received the calls from Coach
Tyack for the play offs our first game
would be Thursday. I have to admit it
seemed far away. So, coach scheduled
a practice for any guys that could make
it before the big game. I talked with Matt
and found out we played his team the
Cincinnati Reds first in the play offs. So,
we had a couple of laughs and promised
each other that the other guy would lose
for sure. I guess we were both feeling
pretty confident. I can tell you this, I can
definitely feel the step up we where all
taking but I don't feel like it is something
we as a team cannot handle. We all
want to stay loose and confident. We
have all been put on this team together
and each guy brings just what we need
to compete and play through the
playoffs. The trust factor is instilled in
each one of us. The coaches have each
brought the details out we needed to
work on all season long and we are
starting to get it. I know with in myself
you have a draw factor. Not sketch like
draw. The ability each of us has to draw
upon your own experience. The sense
you have, to draw upon your teammates

strengths and confidence. You have to draw parallels to situations that you have practiced and see them realized in the game situation. Greatness is beginning to formulate with in each boy. You can't traipse into the playoffs with a chip on your shoulder. You can accentuate what you have learned and know to take advantage of the next game. That is exactly what we plan to bring with us in our arsenal. With that comes the bats that smash the hits, the mitts that snag the line drives and the throws that beat the runner every time. Yet, if I were to draw a picture of a winning heart I would say look at the boy I'm looking at in the mirror. Transformations take place within your heart. They say you can't measure heart. I disagree whole hardily. You can see it in each practice and in each game. You have a passion to make a difference and you see how you take that piece of the puzzle that you represent and it becomes a key play to win that days game. Dreams are made of reflections that outline the willingness to work and make a difference and lead right where you are. So, get the cameras ready, pop your mitts, time your swings, slap your teammate on the back, and give your coach a nod. Whatever you do bring you heart and clear mind and come prepared to play the games of your life that make moments memories forever. That is a little overwhelming to think about. So, I'm out of here, like whatever. We came to practice Tuesday each boy from a little different direction but all for the same purpose in our hearts to win our up coming game. Zack came cruising up on his bike and locked it to the fence. Cody just got dropped off and he was cracking at guys soon as he could. Like it is second nature to him. He always has a sense of encouragement with the remark. What a gift he has. Coach Tyack was rounding us up for a speech on what was a head of us this week. "Guys, I know you have the ability within you, to go far in the playoffs!" said Coach Tyack. "We have clinched our season and that speaks a lot about your character and team work." He exclaimed. "So, take your experience and knowledge and show me one heck of a practice and the next winning game will follow!" said Coach. I could see where he was going and I grabbed my mitt and was ready for some tough grounders at second. He wasn't going to lie back now, nor was it the time to do so. Clearly he had to give us his best to draw out our best and challenge us to rise to the top and beyond. Yeah, the season clinch was really cool to think about but the playoffs are a lesson all to itself. So, the first hit ball from Coach came to me and it took three skips and was leaving some dust behind from the infield and landed in my glove in a dust of smoke. I grabbed the ball out and ripped it to first for the easy out. I heard Coach yell out, "Great job Andrew." Cody had a hard hit which sent him diving to third base and landing on his stomach to snatch the ball but he couldn't turn to get it to the base on time. So, Cody fired it back to Coach at home plate Coach liked the fact that he was able to stop the ball and keep it from going to the out field. Coach worked through every position with solid hits and we looked pretty good I might say. Coach, called us all in, and he grabbed the bucket of balls and we each received ten pitches and that was it. So, we all made the most of them and put into play whatever we could whenever we could. You are transparent and vulnerable to what ever is coming at you. My thoughts could only be centered on making each hit count. I ended up ten for ten with solid line drives grounders and flies mixed in. I could see Dad smiling and nodding as I came in and grabbed my mitt to head back to second base and wrap up the evening until the last batter got his reps in. What a night. The team for the most part mirrored excellence and passion. I didn't see anyone dogging it accept the two dogs at the playground with their master just past center field. No one from the team caught any splinter time on the bench. We were all hustling and making the most even when we were running the bases. Hardly any close calls and mostly good connections through out the balance of the practice. We heard Coach Say, "Great practice guys and we will see you on Thursday night and be ready to measure greatness in the moments and with each pitch." Because the moments lead to the greatness you are reaching for and the world needs to see greatness come from your heart of hearts and it will? So, we all grabbed our stuff and headed for home. Dad ran up and we walked back and he shared, "You made a difference out there as a team and I could see your heart." I looked him in the eye and gave him a nice hug on the way back to the car. I realized the great moment we were sharing and took full advantage and the measure was what I brought each and every game and that was my heart. You bring your heart you bring it all and it is very difficult to match anything up against that when you're sailing so high. I hit the sack as soon as we got home even though school was out. I was bushed and didn't even feel like reading. I felt like I was fast a sleep in a moment and I turned my head and dreamed of winning the playoff.

Well we showed Thursday night we were ready for the Reds. Matt had some nice hits a single and a double. But between Evan with two doubles, Zack four singles, Cody two triples, Danny Haze a home and a triple, I had three straight singles and Sam with two singles we couldn't help but win the game. I went up to Matt after the game and congratulated him on his awesome hits. We put together a nice game and hit Dairy Queen for Blizzards and called a night. What an awesome win and we knew some how the adventure of the play offs were made in the moments and with our hearts pounding all the way.

We lost our next game on Saturday to the Twins. We weren't playing well and they had a pitcher dominate us and were getting a lot of strike calls from the Umpire. One after one he was taking our team apart. When he didn't get us with strikes we seemed to ground the ball right to their infielders and were out as a force. I could see Coach Hayes was upset. The Twins were placing their hits perfectly and beat us five to nothing. We all left that night with certainty that we had to win our next and last game or we would end up in fourth place for the playoffs. Our chance for first or second was diminished today. We couldn't seem to catch a break. The one good thing I could see from my teammates was they didn't hang their heads down or whip their caps into the dirt. We had a passion to win still and that we wouldn't come up short of the third place trophy. We all wanted to play in the World Series for our age group but that was out of our reach with the loss to the Twins. Beaten by the Twins, yet not defeated in our hearts. You can't divide a team from their hearts. After all we have to look in the mirror and face the giants everyday of our lives. Giants that threaten to take the best of us and have us fall short of our goals and lose our hearts. The Diamond Backs were not going to let that happen. The true tests in life are always how you handle the same situation the next time you get a shot to turn destiny around. I can see the best is yet to come. I could see in all my teammates they weren't walking back to the cars with their heads down but up. The parents were surrounding the boys with encouragement and not remorse. So, something was different and would carry us surely to success in our next game on Monday night. We found out just before we left that we would be facing the Cubs for the trophy and third place in the playoffs. So, we would indeed get our second shot to put this season straight and defeat the Cubs which would be the goal we just came up short in our earlier meeting. The Cubs-we can beat these guys and we will beat these guys. We have to look ahead and know within each of us lies greatness and that greatness may not determine our future but who we are. Though the hats may change next seasons and the guys as well. At least we can hang our Diamond Back hats on this, we have heart.

Chapter 16
Courage To Win

With the Saturday game we had to short a turnaround to fit a practice in before we played the Cubs on Monday night. So, we had to show up with our A game tonight. I jumped out of the back seat of the car ready with my baseball bag, bat and baseball glove and balls. I pulled on my Diamond Backs baseball cap and gave it a tug down just above my eyes. I slung my bag over my shoulder and headed for the baseball field behind Sundling Junior High School for the game of my life. I was determined in my heart of hearts I was ready to play and win this game. I wouldn't say I wasn't nervous but I compartmentalized any fear and just look forward to playing baseball and winning the game. I know we are going to win the game. I have visualized it all weekend and went over our roster and our toughness. Not to mention our ability from the top off the line up to the bottom it is seamless. We are not lacking in one area. I can't see any scenario where the game ends up any other way. I could see from the other guys on the team arriving they seem to have the same confidence I was feeling. Coach Tyack seemed nervous and so did Sam. I went over and gave Sam a nod and a wink to let him know we had this game and season wrapped up. We all know you have to play the game. We went through warm ups each guy paired off to throw and stretch out just like Coach Hayes taught us. The Cubs were warming up on the field. It was looking pretty obvious we wouldn't get on the field to game time. I lined up with Cody who was really firing the ball in there from what I could feel from the after shock. Somehow you fight through it and fire it right back at him too. After tossing the ball Cody admitted I was stinging his hand through the glove when it popped his mitt. I smiled to myself and got ready for the game. Sam was our team captain went out with the coaches to get the umpires rules and boundaries. Wow, we were about to get this game rolling after all. My heart was pounding and I could see I would be batting fifth in the line up. The game started and the Cubs were up first. We went through their first three guys like butter. Evan was awesome. Evan was up first then Zack, Cody, Danny and then myself. The pitcher didn't have very good control because he didn't pitch all the time. His Dad was the coach of the Cubs. I knew Jack from school but his pitches were coming in on arch. He walked our first two batters Evan and Zack. So, we had men on first and second. Cody came up and hit a liner to the short stop who made a great jump up to catch the line drive but our guys got back to their respective bags on time. Danny hit a nice hit over the third baseman and we had the bases loaded. I came up to bat ready to give it my all. Jack gave me the perfect pitch and I hit the ball over the short stop for a double and scored Evan and Zack and had Danny at third base. We were suddenly up two runs and I could hear our parents cheering and I looked straight down at second base to get my head back in the game. Sam came up and ripped another double and scored Danny and I and we went up four to nothing. I looked back toward third and I could see Coach Tyack clinching his fist and smiling at his son Sam who asked for time at second to get set. Joe came in and hit Sam in with a strong double to right field and we went up five to nothing. Our bench was getting pretty fired up and we were leaning and yelling through the chain link fence encouragement to our teammates. Brian and Adam came up and both struck out. We went out to the field and I took second base this inning. We went through the next three guys like butter, again. Evan was on and we could tell the first three innings we would coast through if he continued like he was. The second and third innings seemed like we were going through the motions as Evan went three up three down in the respective innings. Yet, we would get men on and couldn't score any more either. No matter how hard we tried the score was five nothing. Zack came in the fourth and was perfect too. He went through Dakota, Shoe and Jack with out scoring one run. The fifth inning we went through our best guys two and two were out on double plays and a liner up to the first baseman who tagged our guy out. Wow, that was Zack, Cody and Danny. I could see Coach Hayes was in disbelief. In the bottom of the fifth our lead was dwindling away. Zack, are pitcher was getting clobbered by Dakota, Shoe and Jack and their coaches went wild. The score was five to three. Before long we totally lost our lead. The score was suddenly tied five to five by a two run homer from their sixth man up. The Cubs were screaming and the game was getting out of hand. Coach Tyack switched Danny and Zack and Danny went on to get the next three outs we needed. Danny was the ultimate closer. Talk about cruise control for a baseball team but we were always alert because you just never know what can happen. After all we were up five nothing. The sixth inning I was starting to feel the pressure. I came up to bat and was ready to be the difference maker. The first pitch was a strike and the second one was a strike too. The third pitch came in and I hit it strong over the first baseman's head and I was safe at first. Our next batter was Sam and I stole second base and I was safe. I stole third base on the next pitch and just got there in time. Shoe from the Cubs had a terrific throw. Sam popped out to the second baseman Jack and we had one out. Joe hit a ball straight to the second baseman and he was safe a first. Coach Hayes was holding me at third. I didn't like the idea of this game going any more innings. I was praying for Brian to get a solid hit and score me. Brian came up and hit the first pitch to right field and their fielder was lined up perfect for the catch, which he did. I turned back and touched third base and took off for home. I could see my buddy Dakota from The Cubs parked perfectly just in front of home plate. The throw was coming in and I dove face first on my stomach and took my slide slightly behind home plate and I could see Dakota made the catch and was coming around for the tag. Just before he tagged me I touched the back of the plate and the umpire called me safe. I stood up and before I knew it my teammates came running and were jumping up and down and lifted me over their heads. I realized we won the game. I never felt such joy. Our parents were just crazy. Coach Tyack brought a cooler over with white grape juice packaged in green champagne like bottles for every guy. We cracked them open and were spraying and drinking the white grape juice with all the boys on the team. Not even one minute after we started the celebration the sky opened and it began pouring rain. We grabbed our baseball stuff and ran back to our parent's cars for cover. The celebration was cut short outside but continued in our van before we left. Mom, Dad and Hannah were high fiving me and I we were totally soaked but it didn't seem to matter at the moment. My Dad was calling his parents on the phone to share the game winning details. What an amazing ending to our season and we ended up In Third Place for the playoffs for our age group. The next Saturday Coach Tyack invited the guys and the families over for a softball game and a cook out. I remember laughing with the guys in their living room and just being guys. We had a blast. Not to mention the fun of watching our Dads over run the bases and looking old. Even Hannah was having fun to with the other younger brothers and sisters. We had our Trophy Ceremony the next Saturday and we received a t-shirt that was printed Division Champs. Our First Place Trophy for the season. Finally our Third place Play Off Trophy. The Coach Tyack announced our names and stated a fun memory about each guy and gave us the Trophies. What an amazing day. We gathered for a few minutes and took some team pictures together. I remember my parents taking a picture of Hannah and I together which captured the greatness of the entire day. She is an awesome supportive sister and came to all my games.

I have experienced a lot of great times in my life as I have grown up. I seem to forget how difficult the journey can be for me at times. I have been through the joys of seeing people I love, my first couple birthdays, my first movie and pulling in the parking lot and screeching. I will never forget the joy of taking off for home and reaching for a goal that I was uncertain of the outcome at best. I came through the experience victorious with my team. I look at my Dad and I realize I found, The Courage To Win.

First printing

All characters appearing in this work are
fictitious. Any resemblance to real
persons, living or dead, is purely
coincidental.

ISBN: 978-0-615-25662-7
Published By SDS Publishers
At LULU.com
www.lulu.com

Printed in the United States of America

www.ingramcontent.com/pod-product-compliance
Lightning Source LLC
Chambersburg PA
CBHW030345030726
47499CB00003B/906